Visionary Tales

for the

New Earth

by

Nadja

NadjaMedia.com

Nadja Media
530 Los Angeles Ave., Suite 115
Moorpark, California 93021

ISBN-10: 1942057032
ISBN-13: 978-1-942057-03-1

This is a work of fiction. Names, characters, places, and incidents either are a product of the author's imagination or are used fictitiously, and any resemblance to actual persons, living or dead, business establishments, events, or locales is entirely coincidental. The author of this book is not a medical doctor and does not dispense medical advice or prescribe the use of any technique as a form of treatment for physical, emotional, or medical problems without the advice of a physician, either directly or indirectly. No liability is assumed for damages resulting from the use of or misinterpretation of information contained herein. The information is meant as a guideline only and to help Humanity better reflect upon themselves, where they have been, where they are now, and where they potentially may be going. Nadja never advocates the use of violence in any form.

Dedication

This is a collection of timeless stories that will resonate with your soul and warm your heart. Dedicated to all those looking for hope, inspiration, freedom of Spirit, unity, and peace. From my inner child to yours.

— Nadja

Acknowledgments

With gratitude for the heart-centered ability to Listen and Create which has been bestowed upon all of us by the Source of All.

Introduction

Discover herein a compilation of new myths or fairytales for the New Age, the New Earth. This is a book for the conscious community and children of all ages. The twenty stories will inspire new ideas, bring hope, wonder, and joy into the readers' lives, and open and warm the hearts of all. The stories are magical, transformational, adventuresome, and yet gentle.

Contents

Star Girl

Star Girl wanted to be born in Tibet, high in the sacred mountain peaks of the Himalayas. And so it was. Her parents were weavers. They were simple, pure in heart and mind, worshipped the Source of All That Is, and honored Mother Earth.

From the beginning Star Girl's childhood was unusual. When she slept, her body emanated a gentle pink mist that glowed in the dark. Her parents marveled at this as they watched the ebb and the flow of this seemingly alive substance moving in rhythm with her breath flowing in and out, in and out, in and out.

Star Girl was a happy child. She never lost her Remembering when she came here to join us Earthlings. The minute she closed her eyes at night, she woke up somewhere else in the Universe, to connect and have fun with her Star Family that she had left, to sojourn upon Planet Earth.

As Star Girl developed from babyhood into a youthing, she was a growing source of amazement to her humble parents. When she slept at night, she emitted the most ecstatic Music. Her parents thought their hearts would burst as they listened to the glorious sounds coming forth from their sleeping child. The Music was never the same. It was different every night. It was the type of Music that opened and nourished awakening hearts, connecting the listener to the Mysteries held deep within them. These very same Mysteries linked them with the Source of All Creation.

Star Girl's parents gave her complete freedom. They were filled with gratitude that the Source of All elected them to raise her as their very own. Star Girl loved the nighttime most of all. During the early evening she would kiss her parents on the forehead, wave goodbye to them, and start walking barefoot through the beloved mountain peaks of the farthest most reaches of Tibet.

She especially loved the falling stars. Every time she spotted one, she would watch in breathless wonder as it made its quick descent to Earth. She would always return to her home in the wee hours of morning to sleep in her little straw be, woven lovingly by her parents.

Eventually, Star Girl's Star Family awakened her to the knowing that it was now time for her to collect the falling stars. She gasped in excitement as this task resonated to the very core of her Being. They told her it was for this reason that she came to visit Planet Earth. Shortly afterward, she started gathering together some yak wool, handfuls of very colorful, long, narrow ribbons, a few aromatic herbs, and eagle feathers. From this assortment she wove together and fashioned a most exquisite basket. Every day, when the sky started to darken into dusk, Star Girl would kiss her parents on the forehead and leave her home. Her parents would watch her disappear barefoot into the night, carrying her big, beautiful yak wool basket with its colorful ribbons trailing behind her or waving excitedly in the wind.

Stars are like snowflakes in that there are never two the same. They are alive, shimmering and vibrating, singing their own Music. Star Girl could not collect more than 2 or 3 stars in her basket at a time. She was led to a huge underground cavern near where she lived, in which she could keep the stars. The cavern glistened with its crystalline walls and extended for miles upon miles deep down under the Earth's crust. Star Girl loved this Work. You could hear the joyful sound of her laughter, like delicate silver bells, when she saw a falling star and was able to catch it and put it in her basket.

Each night, she would deposit her treasures in particular rooms within the crystalline cavern under the guidance of her Star Family, before she returned home to her little straw bed. This was truly a labor of love. Star Girl performed this task every evening until this Work was complete and it was time for her to leave the Planet. She had virtually collected enough falling stars to create another Milky Way, deep in the bowels of our Beloved Earth Mother.

These stars have been giving forth their Light and singing their Music for years upon years upon years, unbeknownst to Humanity. The time has finally come for us to awaken. When you go to bed at night, call forth Star Girl and it will be her pleasure to guide you to the crystal caverns deep within the mountains of Tibet where you can listen to the Music, meet your Star Family, and receive Knowing, Unconditional Love, and Peace.

All is in readiness.

Ask and you will receive.

Namaste

Music Of The Flowers

There is a story I would like to share with you. It concerns Gremlin, who lived in the forest depths. Now Gremlin was noted for his standoffishness. In fact, no one ever went near his dwelling except Beetle. And even Beetle kept his distance, but was able to observe Gremlin so as to inform us of his doings. For Beetle could disguise himself very well to blend into the foliage, and Gremlin was none the wiser.

Over the years, Beetle grew quite fond of

Gremlin even though there was no communication. You see, Gremlin was a Student of Life. His main interest was flowers. He was studying the color and harmonics of flowers and had found that flowers of one color played variations of one particular tone scale. He would walk into fields of wild flowers and listen to their music. The music was beautiful, indeed, but it was, you might say, uncultivated.

It was Gremlin's pleasure to orchestrate and conduct the Music of the Flowers. He did this by experimenting on several plots of land. He would plant particular flowers in certain formations or designs so that their music would blend into a symphony. Each garden he created played its unique composition. He used darker, larger flowers – particularly those which went way down inside to the nectar, for deep pathos. The lighter and more delicate the flower, the more celestial and etheric was its musical quality.

Gremlin never felt the loss of companionship, for his love of the flowers and their love for him made him very, very happy. Each day, he was eager to try another experiment, planting this one by that one, to see what effect this would have on the music.

At first Beetle used to laugh about Gremlin and everyone had just taken for granted that the elf had gone mad. However, little by little, Beetle began to realize what Gremlin was doing. The more Beetle studied Gremlin the more interested he became. Gremlin had opened up an entirely new vista for Beetle and introduced him to a research project whose only product was pure joy. Gremlin seemed to have a very great reverence for something beyond Beetle's grasp.

At times, Beetle would see Gremlin lift up his arms in praise and gratitude for being able to partake in such joy. Beetle himself would be taken over by a feeling of ecstasy that he was able to observe and begin to understand Gremlin. Beetle could not hear the celestial symphonies, but he did know in part what was going on.

The Others in the village started to notice Beetle change. He was always a very jovial, talkative chap, but he began to get quieter and didn't maintain the whirl of social activities in which he usually engaged. The Others still laughed and joked about Gremlin, but Beetle said they were wrong and just didn't understand.

A desire started growing deep in Beetle's heart and that was to be able to hear the Music of the Flowers. He was impatient with himself, for he felt he was too cumbersome, his shell too hard to be able to really listen. He then began to ask in his quiet moments of solitude that he be shown what he must do to be able to hear Gremlin's symphonies. The only word he received was "Patience."

One day, when Beetle watched Gremlin, big tears of self-pity welled up in his eyes, for he felt he would never ever be able to hear the celestial music. When the tears hit the ground the flowers heard it and the music stopped, for they felt the heavy weight of sadness. Gremlin knew there was something wrong and looked in the direction the flowers told him and there he beheld Beetle, sobbing and practically drowning in tears.

Actually, Gremlin had known all along about Beetle observing him, for the flowers knew all secrets and hid nothing from him. But

Gremlin, being gentle and wise, did not want to intrude upon Beetle's game. At last, he was able to speak with Beetle. You see, not only had Beetle grown fond of Gremlin, but also Gremlin had become very compassionate toward Beetle over the years.

Gremlin went over to Beetle and comforted him. Beetle just about dissolved in tears for not being able to hear the music and in joy for having at last been "discovered" and able to talk with Gremlin, who he now considered his closest friend.

Gremlin finally got it out of Beetle what he was crying about and said, "Why, Beetle, anyone can hear the Music of the Flowers if they have a strong desire. Their music flows through your heart of hearts, or the deepest part of your heart. Do not listen with your ears but listen with your heart. Open your heart."

"But how do I do that?" sobbed Beetle. "You do that by practicing patience, love, and gratitude. Be patient with all things, be thankful for all things, and understand that behind all illusion is Divine love," answered Gremlin.

"Oh, thank you, Gremlin. I shall do as you say and one day I hope to hear what you hear."

"You will never hear what I hear and I will never hear what you hear, for each heart reflects the Glory in a different manner, but all who hear the music are filled with joy and ecstasy. The only one who can hear what each of us hears with our heart of hearts is God. For you see, we are the flowers in His Garden."

With that Beetle departed and began to practice the art of opening his heart. Each day he felt a slight part of himself fall away. Surely the door to his heart had rusted shut and he would have to exercise great patience in its gradual opening. Beetle endured many trials and tribulations, for he knew that the work he was now doing was more meaningful than any he had ever done.

As his Door was opening, Beetle went through some remarkable changes. He penetrated unknown depths of his Being and began to get glimpses of the Whole of Life. Many times he became weary, so weary that he would lose the desire to go on anymore, but nonetheless, on he went and passed into higher levels of understanding. Beetle worked in this manner for several years. Gremlin was pleased with his growth and encouraged him by relating his own stories of the difficulties he had in opening his Door.

At last, one day when Beetle was in the Garden, he began to hear strains of the most indescribably beautiful music. It came quietly.

Its magnificent grandeur had a soothing effect and Beetle was filled with serene ecstasy. Gremlin was overcome with gratitude that he had been given the opportunity to help another to Listen. Beetle looked around him and for the first time saw that the flowers were not flowers at all, but only expressions of music. He then realized that he, Gremlin, and the Others were also expressions of music, each one playing at a different vibratory rate. Everything was alive with the Sound and shimmering in Golden Light. He suddenly understood that the only thing wrong with the world was that no one listened to the music anymore. In fact, they had forgotten all about it.

Gently, Gremlin took Beetle's hand and said, ''My Brother, I love you with all my heart. Let the music guide you always.''

Beetle was filled with a deep and abiding

peace. He felt at one with all creation. He cherished this moment in time and wished it could last forever. However, he knew there was much to be done.

He hugged Gremlin and looked deeply into his eyes and said, "Thank you. I will carry you in my heart wherever I go."

With that Beetle turned and walked slowly away down the path. Gremlin watched him disappear from sight and then picked up his hoe and returned to his Work.

Portals

Open the Door

Open the Gate

Lay down your burdens

Lay down your hate

Take up the Staff

Take up the Power

Walk into the Garden

Each moment

Each hour

Otto
The Sandman

Even when Otto was young, he wanted to be a scientist. He read all he could find on the subject and studied everything around him very carefully—weighing, measuring, calculating, and making up theories, postulates, and conclusions.

He carried home armloads upon armloads of books. While other children were playing baseball, jumping rope, and playing tag, Otto was wearing a path between the library and his house. He would sit hour after hour in his room reading, hidden by towers of books piled upon books. Oftentimes his parents had trouble locating where he was in the room.

They would stand at the door and yell down the various corridors of books, ''What are you doing, Otto?''

''Searching,'' he always answered.

Needless to say, he was very bright, but in school, he hardly ever paid attention to anything, for he was too busy dreaming up new problems to work on. In fact, his teachers thought him a rather dull child.

He knew he wanted to investigate and explore something that no one else had, or at least to the depth he was willing to go. He spent years picking and discarding many possible subjects. Finally, he decided upon grains of sand.

To begin this study, Otto had to make up a suitable vocabulary. He had read enough scientific literature to know how to concoct names and then Latinize them. His words were very impressive, indeed, and most of them were near impossible to pronounce. This made his work acceptable to the scientific community. Once, he wrote a paper describing just the physical features of a grain of sand. It was so full of technical words and a few formulas that it was selected for publication in one of the leading scientific journals. Actually, what he wrote was so simple that it could have been put into one small paragraph, but his paper made it all very proper, very complex, and only understood by scientists, and then only those familiar with his terminology.

Otto was much encouraged by all this and spent his days studying all he could about his subject. He built a laboratory at the beach where he never ran out of specimens. His laboratory kept expanding, for he was attempting to categorize sand grains. This was an exceptionally difficult task, as they were similar to snowflakes in that they were each so different.

Up to this time, Otto had separated each individual sand grain into a special compartment, which made his laboratory resemble the honeycomb of a beehive—only the compartments were far smaller. There was one occasion when Otto found 20 similarities between two grains. He was ecstatic for this breakthrough and therefore he had one compartment, and only one, with two grains of sand in it. Otto was a very careful and thorough scientist and listed about 500 characteristics of sand grains. He was waiting for the day when he would discover a grain of sand that was exactly like another on all 500 points.

So much sand disappeared from the beach into Otto's laboratory that the citizens expressed concern. By now Otto was very famous and people came to visit him from around the world. He was considered the most outstanding member of the community on account of this. However, it was decided that the mayor must call upon him and forbid him to remove any more of the beach. Otto was so intent on his work that he never realized he had removed over half the beach into his lab and that he was actually upsetting the ecology and scenery of the environment.

It wasn't until the mayor spoke to him about it that he realized what he had done. Sure enough, Otto looked around and saw he was creating an ugly mark upon the town's scenery.

He felt terrible about this oversight. Usually, he had eyes only for sand grains and was now surprised to notice how beautiful the sky and sea were and how the birds flew between them through the sun rays.

Otto agreed with the mayor and apologized for disturbing the natural beauty. He even thanked the mayor in the name of science, for now he would be forced to examine sand grains from another area. He had been meaning to do this but it was far too easy for him to gather specimens where he was living. Now he could compare two areas.

It didn't take long for Otto to discover another spot. It was outside the city limits and there he began again hauling sand grains. He kept accurate records by putting different colored dots on each compartment, signifying respectively what locality the sand grains came from, how deep they were in the sand, how close they were to the water, if they were found on a hill or in a hollow, ad infinitum. All this detailed work caused him at times to wish he had chosen a simpler subject or at least one that could be narrowed down—for example, the uppermost dot on the right wing of the Monarch Butterfly.

Otto began to collect samplings here and there. He found this a simpler method. He discovered that there were over a million types of sand grains that shared no characteristics or combinations of characteristics. There were other grains, which shared one to 450 similarities with others. One time he found a sand grain, which had 487 characteristics in common with another, but he was always looking for two that were exactly alike.

At the World Symposium on Science, Otto

announced that he had found two sand grains that shared 490 characteristics and that he would spend the rest of his days trying to find at least one sand grain exactly like another. He asked for world cooperation for this project and scientists from several warring countries actually shook hands with one another and with Otto, making peace in this united effort. There was great applause and Otto was awarded medals.

He was proud of his medals but all he really cared about was his research project. After he returned home to his laboratory, he began to get sand samples from all over the world. He was thrilled but he had to write back long letters to get all the correct information which people in their haste did not supply him. By the time his letters reached them, most of the people couldn't even remember where they had found the grains, so Otto had to discard a good many of them. He remained first and foremost a scientist.

His laboratory continued growing. It grew up in the air and over the land and became almost a city. Everyone who lived nearby was very impressed because of its size and also because they couldn't understand what Otto was talking about, for he used such long, complicated words. In fact, they sometimes thought he was speaking a foreign language, except he did use words and phrases like: "hello, goodbye, thank you, to be sure, for example, you see," etc. People would smile and nod and wait for Otto to finish what he had to say and when he said, "Goodbye," they knew for sure he had finished and they would shake hands and then depart.

Two words could describe Otto—diligent

and devoted. In his search, he invented a microscope, which could be used only for sand grains. It was shaped like a round ball so all sides of the grain could be magnified at the same time. He secured a patent for it but he really didn't have to, for he was the only one world over who was that interested in sand grains. No one else even wanted one.

Otto built a special room in his laboratory, which he called his quiet room. Whenever he had an especially difficult problem he would go there. No one else but Otto was ever allowed in this space. The room was very simple in design. The walls were blue. At the top of the room, there was a window from which Otto could look up and see the sky. In the center of the room was a glass case in which stood a small platform covered with purple velvet, on the top of which was a grain of sand (one of the most beautiful he had ever seen) mounted on his microscope. In this sanctuary, he would get new ideas, insights, and answers to problems.

One day, when Otto was in this silent place looking at his sand grain, he became very discouraged. "Why can't there be two exactly alike? Why? I've wasted my entire life trying to prove something I know nothing about. Something greater than I am must hold the answer. I know many things but they are truly nothing—just facts, unrelated facts. Surely there is an answer. I'm missing something so huge I cannot see it. It escapes me. I truly give up!"

"Are you absolutely sure?" a deep voice echoed throughout Otto's sanctuary.

"W-w-w-w-where are you?" stammered Otto.

"Oh, you cannot see me. Please calm yourself. I am here to assist you. I was just waiting for you to reach the end of your resources—to surrender. Now, I think you are ready to learn.'' ''I don't understand. First, you're invisible and second you can help me when I am the only scientist in the world working on this project? How so?'' asked Otto.

''Otto, I know you are sincere in your desire to analyze sand grains but you were correct when you said you were missing a huge piece of the puzzle. That is what I will show you, but I could not step in until you had exhausted all of your human methods, which took about 20 years of your concerted effort.''

''I was so sure I would find the answer. I was so excited going through the process but I now realize I have failed miserably. I do not understand what you could possibly do for me,'' said Otto tearfully.

''Otto, you did not fail. The work you

accomplished was a gargantuan task and you approached it with gusto and tremendous discipline. It was a huge undertaking and you learned many things. However, you just did not achieve your final goal. I am only allowed to help people when they have put forth maximum effort, have exhausted all possibilities, and then give up. For up to this point, they would be unwilling to take another's direction.

Let's try this from an angle you were not capable of achieving on your own. Are you ready?"

Otto's heart was thumping—so close to his goal and yet could he trust this voice? What did he have to lose?

"Absolutely!" Otto responded. He felt he was being guided by a friend, a very intelligent, but invisible friend.

"Now, Otto, you must follow my direction

down to the smallest detail. Just stay seated and concentrate on the sand grain in the glass case. You will feel yourself getting very tiny. Don't worry. It's only an illusion—as is everything else,'' the voice chuckled.

Otto felt himself getting very, very small. He knew something miraculous was about to happen. The next thing he knew, he was standing in front of the sand grain. He looked way up. To him, it appeared like a cathedral with very tall, shiny walls which caught the light rays and bounced them back with the most exquisite colors. He couldn't even see the top. Slowly he walked up to the wall facing him and touched it. A door opened and he walked in.

''Wow,'' breathed Otto. He had never used the word since way before he learned to read (at about 2 years of age). ''Wow,'' was all he was able to say, for up he looked—up, up, up, and all he could see for as far as eternity were stars; but they were different ones from the earth. None of the constellations were the same. "Wow," he breathed again and the word echoed out to infinity.

Otto's head jerked as if he had awakened from nodding off in his chair. He was sitting as usual in front of the glass case with the grain of sand mounted on his microscope. However, he knew something changed within him. He became a completely different person. He felt calm, relaxed, and filled with joy. From that day on Otto didn't talk very much, but when he did he used very simple words. His whole vision had changed and he noticed everything around him. He became friendly with others and was interested in what they thought and how they were doing. He always had a smile on his face.

The scientific community no longer invited

him into their circles, for his words were too simple and his actions were child-like, certainly not fitting for a well-known scientist. Otto said in the kindest manner possible that most of what had taken him all those years to research could have been reduced to a sentence or even a word. Upon hearing this, a shudder ran throughout the World Symposium of Scientists.

Otto didn't mind. He had found what he was looking for. He now knew why there were never two sand grains the same and never two anything exactly alike. He approached everything and everyone—every living creature and plant with awe and wonder; for if that is what is in a grain of sand, just think of what is in other things!

The Artist

O nce upon a time, there was a little boy who loved to draw ducks. He rarely drew anything else. Mostly they were imaginary ducks. People would look at his drawings and say, ''How nice,''' or, ''How cute,'' but he knew they were far from what he could draw and that someday he would be a real artist and his ducks would be unique to the world of art.

As he grew and experienced life, he somehow managed to express this in his art.

When his friends laughed at him and pulled his ears, he painted this into his ducks. When his friends loved him and encouraged him, this, too, added a different quality to his ducks. He painted into them his curiosity of life, his adventures, his wonder and love of the seen and the unseen. Each person he met added their unique characteristic to his ducks.

He married. His love for his wife and children, his struggle to communicate—to express the depths, his grappling with the adult world of responsibility continued to add deeper dimensions to his painting.

Becoming mature in life, seeing and experiencing completely different levels of understanding than when he was a child, becoming aware of the simplicity and rhythm of life on a grander scale brought to his ducks an elusive and yet very real quality of Soul.

Now, at last, he felt he was ready to begin painting as an artist. People were captivated by his compositions. They all appeared very simple—a solitary duck—but there was so much content that each painting seemed to have a never-ending fount of understanding. Each one was like a book or a symphony. He compared these paintings to the ones he did as a child and those in his youth. The ducks looked the same but the whole feeling quality was different. Each painting he did was deeper and more meaningful than the last one. He knew he would never stop painting, for he had tapped into the Source. He was now bringing to his art dimensions of mind, heart, and soul that few have ever bothered to probe.

At times he would run across young ones who had a real desire to be an artist. They would ask him for advice. He never mentioned paints, proportion, or line. He only said, ''Paint your life, My Child, and live it fully and deeply. The true artist is a traveler within the Kingdom of the Self. The further you travel, the greater your art. The greater your art, the more fully you express to people who they are. Your work is never done, for no artist has ever expressed totality, but only approached its frontier.''

Dancing the Sacred

Long ago, in the days of ancient Greece, during the time when people would flock to the Oracle of Delphi for guidance and direction in their lives, lived a beautiful woman by the name of Diana. She was a high priestess of the Dance.

Her parents knew she would be a dancer while she was still in her mother's womb. In those days, there were great numbers of people who were highly advanced. They had the ability to communicate on many levels of consciousness and were completely telepathic. It was not uncommon for Beings in the spirit world to contact couples on the Earth plane to discuss the possibility of incarnating through them including the reason they sought them out. This was the process that Diana and her parents experienced before her birth.

Diana and her parents had known each other through ten lifetimes together on Planet Earth as well as on the planet of Venus. In all these incarnations, they took on different roles in their family pod. For example, Diana was her father's wife in the family's incarnation before this one and her mother was their child. These arrangements were made so everyone could have experience with each other through different perspectives.

Diana's family pod were all artists for many lifetimes. Their sensitivities were attuned to the

Higher Frequencies and their creative energy kept increasing and refining within the synergy of each new configuration of the family pod. As Diana made contact with her soon-to-be parents, the family pod felt great joy, for they would shortly be gathered together again to express their artistry and deep love for one another. Diana knew they would provide an environment for her that would be secure, loving, and conducive to artistic development. Her parents understood her life purpose to be a sacred dancer and consented to open up all the channels to help her achieve this goal.

She told them of her travels to far distant galaxies where she was able to expand her dancing abilities and merge with the Celestial Music. She informed them that she wanted to be born in the springtime at night so she could be greeted by the scent of the Sacred Night-blooming Aglaea Lily, which breathed forth its joy during this time each year. It was important to Diana to be able to take this aroma into her small body, as it would activate codes within her that would enable her to connect at the deepest level with the Sacred Dance. Inhaling this flower's fragrance would only work its magic if done immediately after birth.

Of course, Diana's parents were in total agreement with her. Her soon-to-be mother and father had their gardener plant the Sacred Night-blooming Aglaea Lily among the other flowers surrounding their dwelling. They also instructed him to place this sacred flower in the ground encircling the pool in the atrium, which graced the center of their home and into which Diana would be birthed.

During her time in the womb, Diana dreamed magnificent dreams, sharing them telepathically with her family pod. Her mother's body glowed with a shimmering rainbow hue as a result of Diana's Being within her. When it was Diana's time to leave the womb, her birth process was totally without fear. Her mother gave birth to her at night beneath the stars in the sun-heated pool in the atrium.

There was another reason Diana requested an evening birth. It was so that all of her Star Family could be present with her on this special occasion. As she literally swam into the world, the aroma of the Sacred Night-blooming Aglaea Lily entered her nostrils and cast her into cosmic consciousness where she was caught up dancing among the star beings in galaxies far beyond the known universe. While she floated in the warm pool, lovingly held in the arms of her parents, shimmering lights of various colors played over her body, caressing it and charging her aura. The only sounds present were her mother humming a peaceful melody and the water gently lapping the sides of the pool.

Her mother and father watched her reverently, not wanting to disturb her sacred reverie. They held her in their arms. Their eyes never left her face. At last, when she opened her eyes and met the eyes of her parents, they, too, went into a reverie, for Diana's frequency brought the memories flooding back to them of living a glorious life together on the planet of Venus. The life force streaming through Baby Diana's eyes melted away all remaining dross left in her parents' energy fields. Thus, Diana was born completely free of any birth trauma into her beloved family pod now living on Planet Earth.

Diana was born free. Freedom allows the spirit to literally dance in the body. Diana was engaged in the dance before, during, and after her birth. The dance was sacred in early Greece. It was a process of spiritual healing. It was the highest honor and a great responsibility to be chosen to become a sacred dancer. It was known to the wise ones selecting the children for the Dance that Diana would be chosen even before she was born.

The training of dancers began in early childhood. On Diana's eighth birthday, she was taken to a temple to live. While there, master teachers of impeccable morals and high consciousness taught her and other specially selected children how to develop their minds, hearts, bodies, and spirits to the highest levels. There was as much emphasis on developing the mind and spirit as there was in training the body. It was a truly holistic approach.

As the dancers matured, they developed

into highly evolved priestesses and priests with complete mastery of themselves and the Great Mystery. They had full command of the Sacred Music and Living Color as well as of their minds and bodies and could express this with love and precision. They were consciously aware of the spiritual energies and actively worked with these forces, directing them for the greatest good of the audience. When a dancer had, at last, completed the rigorous training and achieved the honor to dance before an audience, a tiny sacred gemstone encircled with a thin gold band was imbedded into their third eye: emerald for females and ruby for males.

The dancers functioned more or less as physicians and intuitive healers. When they came out upon the stage to greet the audience, they could see energetically what all the problems were. These challenges manifested in each person's aura. It was the dancers' responsibility to work as a team to clear the energy field of every person coming to witness their dance. You might say that the dancers performed spiritual surgery.

All the dancers knew one another intimately from their long association and were able to function as a team to accomplish their goal of healing the entire audience. They formed an organic unit. They were telepathic and communicated with each other on all levels. For the most part, the audience was only aware of the dance compositions, which were magnificent and executed with the highest level of artistry. The people were so enthralled with the beauty of the performances that their concentration was of the greatest intensity. This allowed the sacred dancers to send specifically directed light beams from their bodies into the bodies of those in the audience. They would emit these potent, healing transmissions from their spiritual eye (through the gemstone), their throats, palms of their hands, their fingers, solar plexus, heart, crown chakra, and the soles of their feet and toes.

Each specific body part of the dancers was accurately attuned to emit specialized healing rays. The focus of the performers' thoughts would direct these beams to specific people and to precise areas of their being that required balance and healing. When all needed healing was accomplished, the audience reached a catharsis, a type of savasana, and the dance performance was concluded. The people left the presentation renewed, refreshed, and eager to continue on with their lives. In this way, the sacred dancers were able to heal physical, mental, and spiritual illnesses before they developed into more serious forms. The Dance played a significant role in keeping society healthy and productive.

This was to be the true purpose of the Dance from antiquity down to the present time. In the not too distant future, the Sacred Dance will again be activated.

Drummer Boy

Drummer Boy loved to drum. He did not care if he had an audience or not. He was actually living in the world that the drum beats conjured up. He would always close his eyes when he started to play and seemed to go into a type of meditation. A smile would spread over his face and he would drum for hours upon hours without stopping. He seemed to radiate Light from his body as his hands beat out rhythms of varying intensity and volume. When he finished a session, he would glow and his eyes would sparkle. His movements were filled with grace and strength.

When he played drums outdoors, the animals would join him. Hawks would circle high above, hummingbirds would hover near his body, deer and other wildlife would come to watch from a distance, and the trees would sway. Even the lizards would gather around him and remain motionless until he stopped playing. He drummed in rhythm with the Earth, connecting the Breath of All That Is with the pulse, the heartbeat, of Gaia, our Beloved Earth Mother. He married the energies of the Earth to those of the Sky. He drummed renewal. He drummed healing. He drummed vitality. He drummed Wisdom. He drummed Knowing and he drummed Love so deep that it penetrated all Life forms and transported them into ecstasy.

When Drummer Boy drummed, he actually

traveled along ancient timelines where he met drummers who had once lived upon Planet Earth. They beckoned to him to join their huge circle. Carrying out an ancient practice as old as time itself, they drummed and danced the Universal Dance of the Earth People. They drummed throughout time to help balance the energies on the Planet and to keep the frequency high and pure. Their Work was never done. It was performed with joy as a Sacred Task and the drummers were filled with gratitude.

As Drummer Boy played in this ancient drum circle with spirit people representing all the cultures on Planet Earth, he re-established old relationships without uttering a word. The ancient drummers were all dressed in their respective regalia and formed a True Rainbow Drum Circle. Drummer Boy became their representative on Earth, their channel, so to speak. If you listened carefully to his drumming, you could hear drumbeats that were not his, but that accompanied him to perfection.

When people came to join Drummer Boy, he welcomed them and they drummed until the wee hours of morning, and then they left for home to catch up on their sleep. And, Oh, what dreams they had! Most of them dreamt that they were playing their drum in an ancient drum circle. Most of them saw Drummer Boy continuing to play with them. One thing they all had in common when they awoke was that whatever ailed them was healed. They had a spring in their step and a sparkle in their eyes. They were calm, grounded, nourished, and their hearts were full.

The Rainbow Drum Circle is always searching for channels on Mother Earth. They look for drummers who love themselves, cherish their Earth Mother, and want to heal Her and Her inhabitants, and grace them with Peace.

Otter Girl

Otter Girl lived in the Deep Forest among the fern grottoes, streams, pools, and swift moving rivers. The trees were tall, ancient, majestic and the undergrowth was lush and verdant. The earth was spongy and would give way under your body weight. It was filled with layers upon layers of decaying leaves slowly turning into rich, dark, moist humus. There were mushrooms here and there with huge caps shooting up from the forest floor. The sunlight was filtered through the canopy of leaves high overhead as it made its way down to the ground.

Otter Girl loved her home. She spent her days gathering food, playing tag, swimming, and sunning herself on the banks of the streams and rivers. Her body was quick as a wink, nimble, and slippery. She could disappear in seconds, much to everyone's amazement and dismay. Her eyes sparkled with laughter, vitality, and a touch of mischief. Her skin glistened with health and her teeth were pure white. It was difficult to take your eyes off of her beauty. She never harmed another Being and never ever made fun of anyone. Her laughter sprang from an inner joy and the excitement of discovery.

Sometimes she would engage in wrestling matches with animals ten times her size or more, but she was always victorious because she was an accomplished warrior and never lost her focus. Besides, these Beings always felt her love for them, but a contest was a contest, and they used all their strength and skill, but to no avail. No one could outdo Otter Girl.

She loved engaging in chasing and tickling bouts with chipmunks and other small creatures. They would roll around and around on the ground, gasping for breath between the laughter. The laughter would grow to uproarious levels. The gnomes and elves would take the time to hop up upon the mushroom caps to see all the fun and frolic. During Otter Girl's tickling moments, she was surrounded by circles upon circles of an audience so engaged that they couldn't stop laughing, even when it became painful.

Afterward, she would jump up and play tag

or hide-and-go seek. She seemed to have boundless energy. What fun it was to chase Otter Girl and then have her chase you. She usually could outrun everyone and then jump into a stream or river and disappear, only to re-appear behind her chasers and now chase them all over again. What wonderful days and what great fun for everyone. The Plant and Animal Kingdoms would talk about these events with fondness and excitement for long periods of time afterwards.

Whenever a tree fell, Otter Girl was the first one on the scene to give comfort to the fallen one and to all who inhabited her. When anything went wrong in the forest, Otter Girl was there to lead and lend assistance. She was strong, calm, capable, intelligent, intuitive, and blessed with a loving heart. She was known to repair a rip in a mushroom's cap, sew up a torn butterfly's wing, tend to orphaned fledglings, and fend off the enemies of the animal and plant kingdoms. When there was an argument that grew beyond the solving point, the Beings involved were brought to Otter Girl. She was able to trace the problem back to the cause and then heal it.

When someone was going through a difficult time, sadness, great hurt, or loss, Otter Girl would seek them out and stay by their side so they weren't alone in their overwhelm. She offered her friendship and her heart. Many times she would just sit in silence with them until they were able to find their way back to themselves again and to balance. However long it took, and there was never any rush, Otter Girl stayed and gave her most attentive companionship.

Sometimes all that was needed was an arm

around the shoulder, a loving touch on the cheek, a finger to gently wipe away a tear, or to tenderly hold someone's hand. She would listen in silence with her whole heart and hear the person's sobs or words as they released and emptied out. She never offered advice or her own story, for she did not want to interrupt the flow. The person felt totally loved and cherished as they healed. Otter Girl was in touch with her own Deep Wisdom but her Friendship Work was focused on helping the overwhelmed one find their own connection to Source, and with that came their own solution.

Everyone loved Otter Girl and she loved and cherished them all because she first and foremost loved and respected herself and knew who she was. She extended this Knowing to everything else that had life. This was felt to the core by all the denizens of her Forest World.

They cherished her, for they felt her unconditional love for every one of them.

At the end of every day, the dwellers of the forest would gather for music and dancing. They always started off with expressing gratitude to the Source of All Creation for the Gift of Life. Then they danced and played music accompanied by bullfrogs, crickets, owls, and creatures of the dark night. At eventide, Otter Girl would tell bedtime stories and sing lullabies. Her beautiful voice transported all to dreamland. When she saw their Lights emerge from their sleeping bodies and sway with the music, Otter Girl would gently and lovingly tuck them all in bed and give them a goodnight kiss.

Afterward, she would skinny up to the tops of the trees to watch the stars and bathe in the delicious moonlight. Opening up to Universal Energy, she invited the River of Light to flow through all of her meridians. It was in this way that she renewed herself at night and sustained herself during the day in the Highest Frequency she was capable of. This enabled her to create her Magic and transmit her abundant joy to everyone and everything with which she came in contact.

Otter Girl is the symbol for unbridled joy, exuberance, playfulness, and fun. Thank you, Otter Girl. Oh, what we could all learn from you. When you go to the forest, Otter Girl may allow you to have a glimpse of her, but only if you love and cherish Mother Earth, help protect Her and Her children, and do no harm to anyone or anything, including yourself.

Kaleidoscope Kids

Brian was an unusual boy. Even as a small child when he closed his eyes he would see geometric forms of great beauty moving and dancing. Their color and aliveness would entertain him for hours on end. He would laugh and giggle when his eyes were closed. This totally mystified his parents. He tried to explain to them what he saw but they had no understanding and told him never to tell anyone about this for his protection and theirs. Brian found it really hard to believe that other people couldn't see what he could when he shut his eyes. In spite of this, he honored his parents' request and kept his mind movies to himself.

At the age of eight he developed a new talent. He found out about it in the quietude of his bedroom. He was sitting on a chair facing a blank wall when all of a sudden what he had been seeing in his head was projected onto the wall. It came right out of his forehead, his third eye, just like a projector in a movie theater. He was amazed and overwhelmed with excitement. He knew he now had the ability to create movies in his mind that other people could see as well. It was extremely difficult to keep this to himself, especially since many of the movies were very entertaining. He did not want to alarm his parents any more than he already had, so he kept the lid on this new development.

It wasn't until he made friends with Caroline, a cute little girl in his class, that he found out he was not the only person who could do mind movies. One day, when Brian and Caroline were out on the playground, Caroline invited Brian to come with her. They went to the far end of the playground where there was a locked storage shed with blank walls.

"Come on, Brian, let's go to the other side so no one can see us," said Caroline. She yanked his hand and they ran around to the far end of the shed. "Watch this, Brian," she said. Lo and behold Caroline ran a mind movie. Brian was in amazement. She did it exactly the same way as he did—right out of her third eye onto the wall.

"Wow," exclaimed Brian, "How long have you been doing this?"

"For as long as I can remember," said

Caroline, ''But my parents swore me to secrecy for my protection and theirs.''

''Awesome,'' said Brian. ''Watch this,'' he said as he projected his movie onto the same wall.

''Wow,'' said Caroline. ''Do you think we are the only ones who can do this?''

''Well,'' said Brian, ''There's only one way to find out. Let's sign up for the school talent show.''

''I'm game,'' said Caroline. ''Let's practice on the playground every day.''

''Yes,'' said Brian enthusiastically.

They shook hands and ran to get into line before they were counted tardy.

Brian and Caroline found that they could make movies with each other by projecting from their third eyes at the same time. At last, the day of the talent show arrived and Caroline and Brian were so excited they could hardly stand it.

The show was very good. There were many talented young people in their school. When it was finally Brian and Caroline's turn to perform, they sat in their chairs with their backs to the audience facing a huge blank screen. The lights went out and the music began.

The music was projected onto the screen through the third eye of both Brian and Caroline. Everyone loved the music. No one had ever heard it before. Along with the music were amazing colors and shapes swirling and dancing to the rhythm and beat of the composition. After a few minutes of this, a title appeared on the screen with the credits given to Brian and Caroline and the Greatest Movie Maker of All Time, the Creator.

Their movie lasted about 20 minutes. The

crowd went wild. No one had ever seen such a thing or even known it was possible. As Brian and Caroline turned to face the audience, the crowd gave them a standing ovation. The applause was deafening. The cat was out of the bag.

These movies were fabulous, in living color, and never the same. Brian and Caroline were in great demand. They ended up on TV. Their parents became their managers. They were flooded with so many requests that it would take years to fulfill all the engagements. Brian and Caroline traveled with their parents in a large motor home performing and enjoying huge successes. They were invited to other countries since no one else on the planet could do what they did. They loved doing mind movies on what peace on the planet would look like—the restoration and return of all the inhabitants to a state of vibrant health, bliss, and freedom for all.

Mind movies are so much better than TV, movies in theaters, and the Internet. They are exciting creations that are sourced from within. Try it.

A Knower

Mangusha was a dreamer. However, the dreams he dreamed became reality. He was born centuries ago on the continent of Africa into a tribe called the Monwawa, which means The Inheritors of the Light. He was the son of the king of the tribe who came from a long lineage of royalty. When Mangusha entered the Planet from his mother's womb, his body was encircled with Light that infused his whole being and radiated outward. Just his presence in a room made all the people happy and whole. He laughed a lot and his eyes sparkled and danced with the Joy of Life.

When his parents took him outside, he loved communicating with all the plants, animals, rock people, and nature spirits. His heart danced and he would sing songs. As he sang, a colorful mist would emanate from his mouth and intermingle with anything and everything that surrounded him. Even the so-called inanimate objects sprang to life. The sounds he emitted activated the molecules or source fabric of everything.

Every day the people sought him out. The gift he gave them was always pure joy. They loved life, but from the day of Mangusha's birth they danced their lives with ecstasy. It was similar to a beehive where the bees cluster around the queen bee to receive nourishment, energy, and absorb knowledge.

Mangusha grew into a handsome young man. His bronze body was sleek, fit, and moved with grace. He spent the greatest portion of his days and nights dreaming dreams of cosmic proportions. He loved creating universes where Earthlings could travel to, play, enjoy, learn, and replenish. He never spoke of this to anyone, but it was his passion, his joy. His people loved him even more with each passing year. As they looked into his eyes, which were like deep, bottomless pools of love, their hearts would melt and they would want to do only good for the world and its inhabitants, for they felt the depths of unconditional love to their very core.

Mangusha knew that he was just a mirror for the divinity within all beings. To him they were all miraculous, unique reflections of the

Creator, but he knew he could not trespass upon their secret game of forgetting who they truly were -magnificent Beings cut off from their Knowing. Wherever Mangusha traveled, crowds gathered around him. Many gifted him with their worldly treasures, which he received graciously but had no use for.

It concerned him greatly that people turned to him for their learning rather than going inward to connect up with The Great Universal Wisdom as he did. However, he knew and accepted that this was the way it was and would be until the Time of Great Change which he saw happening in the far, far distant future.

Mangusha would often go away into the mountain wilds to just Be and go deep within to the Inner Beauty, Joy, and Knowing that nourished his whole being. Every time he returned to his village, the people would gather around him and dance in ecstasy. Each time he came back, he would emanate a new frequency, which they couldn't hear, but in their heart of hearts, they felt the tremendous outpouring of Love and their bodies were totally given to the Dance of the Holy.

The Dance would last for days. No one slept or ate, for they were being nourished by a nectar that was so sweet it was almost unbearable, thus the body had to dance the energy out. It was too much to contain within their being. Every time the Dance took place, the village burst into springtime. Everything blossomed, recreated, and bore fruit.

Eventually, as Mangusha's time to leave his body for the Higher Realms was drawing closer, he grew concerned, for the people in his village worshipped him as a god. They depended upon him for their well being.

Already plans were underway to build a ceremony and a teaching about him after his so called death.

He tried to explain to the people that this would be of little use and that this just was not the Way. He knew there was no such thing as death, only a change of form. Nonetheless, after he left them, they continued to worship him for generation upon generation upon generation. However, the Living Frequency was absent and Mangusha was the last person to be born into his royal lineage.

Nadja,
The Rainbow Lady

Nadja, The Rainbow Lady, was engrossed in perfecting her project for the Festival of the Arts, an annual event in the City of Shem. In this city, all the inhabitants were artists and they all participated in the festival. It marked the culmination of their artistic growth and exploration for each year.

Shem had developed to the point where its citizenry did not need to make money, for they could manifest nourishment, shelter, and clothing through the power of their thoughts. If someone wanted to have a different home, he would create the image in his mind and then project it into reality. They devoted all their time and energy to their respective art projects. Consequently, everything flourished and everywhere positive energy was felt and manifested—all worked in harmony. Everyone was free to express his or her creativity. No one was thwarted.

Nadja had spent most of her lifetime investigating the properties of color. Shortly after she came into being, she played with color like Earthling children play with toys. Early in her youth, she discovered ways to extract color along with the aroma from flowers. She then spent years trying to create a full bodied living color that vibrated and scintillated with life and would be able to reproduce itself. Nadja's project had attracted a lot of attention, for color was of great interest to everyone in Shem.

In her youth, during the Festival, she would select brilliantly colored flowers and extract their color and aroma while on stage. She would then perform a dance and scatter the color among the audience. However, the color would not last. In fact, it would begin to fade almost immediately. Through the years she was able to develop her method so that colors would never fade, and this year, at last, she found a way for color to reproduce itself as a separate entity. No one knew of this, for the Festival was a time of great surprise and rejoicing, a time of unveiling and truly a grand celebration.

When the day of the Festival arrived, the citizenry started pouring into the outdoor arena and stage. Gardens and fountains were interspersed among the seats —the natural beauty was breathtaking. When all were ready, a reverent hush fell upon the audience as each one participated in a Silent Dedication to the Creator of All. There was a oneness and a feeling of great peace and joy.

There were many categories of art represented: music, dance, drama, writing, drawing, painting, weaving, architecture, fashion design, horticulture, culinary masterpieces, etc. The Festival lasted approximately four days. The energy level was so high that people did not tire out, but became recharged and renewed.

Nadja's art did not fit into any category. It was unique and could not be labeled, for it was continually changing. At last, it was Nadja's turn to display her creation. She was clothed in a very simple, flowing gossamer tunic, held to her body with a thin, string-like belt braided of pure gold. Upon her head was a garland of flowers and hanging from her shoulder was a pouch supported by another gold band similar to her belt. There was no applause, as the inhabitants of Shem communicated telepathically, exchanging vibrations instead of words, thereby creating an atmosphere of acceptance and love. As she stood there facing the audience, she felt the infilling from her people and they received her love for them.

Nadja reached into her small pouch and scooped up a shimmering mass of liquid color. As she took her hand out of the pouch, she could feel the electricity in the air. She then proceeded to fling the living color from her hand upon the stage as if she were sowing seeds. It looked as if a rainbow sprang out of her hand. Immediately, as each drop fell upon the stage, it grew into a tree. Each tree was different, each one exquisite, producing music which merged into a glorious symphony. Flowers burst forth from each tree and were quickly transformed into luscious fruit, which Nadja proceeded to pluck and place into bowls to pass throughout the audience. When there was enough for all, the trees stopped producing. The audience was spellbound. They had never witnessed anything like this before.

Each year, the best works of art were selected to be displayed in the museum. Nadja's work with living color was one of those selected. The Council of Shem, composed of a group of elders, the Wise Ones, asked her if she would consider taking an assignment to go to Planet Earth to sow her music trees. At first, Nadja could not stand the thought of leaving her home and taking up residence on a planet where many of the inhabitants tried to destroy beauty and lived almost like wild beasts. She did not want to go, but she knew her art was needed there.

After deep consideration and a touch of sadness, she consented to go. As she was nearing the Earth's atmosphere, the heaviness and sorrow was almost more than she could bear—the ignorance was overwhelming. The major factors leading to this tragic situation were greed and selfishness. The natural beauty of the Earth, the animals and plants over which man was given dominion, were being destroyed at an astounding rate by this blindness.

Nadja, at last, touched the Earth's surface. She was able to disguise herself in an invisible shield, as Earthlings would be prone to capture her and put her away in one of their chambers of darkness. Nadja was over 12 feet tall and dressed in the same tunic outfit she wore at the festival in Shem. She had much to accomplish and set out upon her journey by taking long strides and reaching into her enchanted pouch of living color and spilling it upon the hungry earth.

Almost instantly, the trees grew and produced flowers of tropical splendor and intoxicating aroma. Soon after, fruit appeared and music issued forth from each tree. However, the music could not be heard by human ears, but it could be felt and sensed and people were drawn to the trees in this manner. In about a month's time, Nadja's task was completed. She traveled night and day without stopping. She would never have come except for a sense of duty. She did not feel Earthlings were ready but she obeyed the Wise Ones. Her duty done, she sped home at the speed of thought, back to her beloved Shem and her Work on Living Color.

As people on Earth were drawn to the trees

and tasted of their luscious fruit, they seemed to become transformed. They began to hear the wisdom within their hearts. Those changed stopped participating in the madness —being cruel and mean to each other, creating things and working at jobs that would harm humanity, pollute the environment, and dishonor Mother Earth. Somehow they found one another and began restoring Beloved Gaia to her pristine blueprint.

When Nadja returned to Shem, the Wise Ones greeted her with radiant light and the message: "Well done, My Child, well done." Nadja's pouch of living color never ran dry. Little did she know how useful it would be to other planets in the universe when their inhabitants lost their way and needed help to connect with the Wisdom once again.

The Potter

When Jared was a toddler, he loved to play in the dirt. He especially enjoyed making mud and letting it ooze through his fingers. He took to fashioning mud pies and laughing great belly laughs of joy as he threw them back onto the earth and heard them make a loud splat. After a few years of this activity, he began to create small figures of animals out of the mud and let them dry in the hot sun. They became his toys. He would name them and play with them for hours on end.

Jared was happiest when he was outside in the warm embrace of the natural world. He was drawn to animals and developed a friendship with them. They never ran from him in fear, but instead, they seemed to sense his love for them. In fact, when he came upon them, they usually would take a long look at him as if they were speaking and then calmly return to whatever they were doing. They felt completely safe around him.

As Jared grew into a young boy, his friends would bring him their sick animals. He received them with open arms. He loved and cared for them tenderly. After a few days, they would recover and their owners would be overjoyed. Word spread far and wide about the young boy "animal doctor." Soon there were too many animals dropped off for Jared to "cure." He realized that he would either have to turn animals away or learn a quicker method of healing.

He appealed to the angelic realm to help him solve this problem. Lo and behold, after this, the animals only had to be in his presence to experience a total, spontaneous healing. It gave him such joy to share in this Work. Jared was filled with gratitude that he did not have to turn even one animal away. It caused him great pain to see any animal suffer. As Jared developed into a young man, his concern for the suffering of any being grew more intense.

He took up the study of pottery. Ever since he was a kid he felt drawn to Mother Earth and Her bounty. The soil was his first love, so being a potter was no surprise. He loved slapping the clay down on the potter's wheel. He felt the same joy as he did when he threw mud pies as a toddler. He would become completely absorbed as he worked with the clay, giving it form as it whirled its way into the world. This art form satisfied his desire to create beauty and gave him time to think deep thoughts and let his spirit soar. As he became more acquainted with different techniques, he started making beautiful ceramic bowls. Each one was unique; each one was fashioned with love. The number of bowls started to grow beyond his ability to store them. He began giving them away and the people cherished them.

One day one of his best friends, David, became ill. The illness did not go away. The diagnosis was that it was terminal. Jared was overcome by grief that his good friend was so ill that there was no hope for his survival. In fact, Jared was so distraught he stopped creating until one night he had a dream. In the dream, one of the pets that was healed through him, a beautiful brown and white rabbit, came to him and told him to make a special bowl for David and to put into it everything he used to heal the animals.

When Jared awoke, he was like a new person, renewed in Spirit. He had a purpose, a mission to heal his good friend. He prepared the clay and started his potter's wheel. He threw the clay on the wheel and began giving it shape with his hands. As the wheel circled round and round, Jared saw David becoming well, then thriving, and returning to his natural state of vibrant health. As his hands formed the bowl, Jared began singing a Spirit Song that was being given to him from the Great Beyond. It was a song of hope, of healing, and of unconditional love, specific to the blueprint and receptor cells of David's body and spirit. Jared did not know what language was coming through him, but he did know beyond all uncertainty that his friend would be totally healed.

After the bowl was taken from the wheel and completely dried, Jared prepared the glaze with which to decorate it. He gathered healing herbs for their pigmentation and added essential oils for a special touch. As he painted the glaze on the bowl, his hands guided by the Great Artist, he called forth the nature spirits and angels to add their vibration as well. After the bowl was fired and removed from the kiln, Jared marveled at its beauty, for it was a co-creation of many Beings made specifically for his friend, David.

At last, Jared was ready to take the bowl to his sick friend. He called David and told him he wanted to bring him a special gift he had made. David was delighted and asked him to come the very next day. The following day, Jared paused at David's door, whispering a prayer before he knocked. David's mother opened the door. She looked worried and tense. She welcomed Jared and led him to her son's room. When Jared saw David, he had to choke back the tears. His friend was in bed and looked thin and very weak. He was wasting away quickly. David opened his eyes and smiled seeing Jared in his room. They had missed each other a lot.

"Hi, David, it's so good to see you. It's been way too long," said Jared, as he gently placed his bowl on David's nightstand next to his bed. "This was created just for you, David. Please make sure it stays in this spot near you." Jared knew that David did not have the strength to move the bowl but wanted to make sure that David's mother or other visitors would just leave it right by his bedside.

"Gee, thanks, Jared. It's so good to see you. Wow, the bowl is so cool," said David softly. Jared could tell that David was getting tired. It took great effort for him to speak. This was a big change from when they used to talk with each other for hours and hours at a time. They talked a short time longer until David's mother told Jared he must go.

That night, David slept so deeply and dreamed that the nature spirits and angels were singing to him and dancing around his bed. When he woke he felt so much better. His appetite returned. Color started coming back into his face and his eyes started to glow with life again.

One night, David woke up before dawn and saw that the bowl was glowing and actually pulsing with Light. He couldn't be sure but he thought he heard music radiating from the bowl. He definitely felt the music but he couldn't stay awake. David gradually became better and eventually made a complete recovery against all odds. The doctors just scratched their heads and called it a miracle, but David and Jared knew better.

Jared, the Potter, continued on with his Work. The beauty of the bowls was that they never lost their magic and never would. The bowls were actually Spirit bowls, radiating their love out into the world for eternity. Even if they broke into pieces, each piece continued to bring healing and blessings to Planet Earth. The bowls healed many of their maladies and continue to do so up to the present time.

Pure Crystal

Anne Marie knew that somewhere she would find her true love, her other half, her soulmate. She was young, ripe, and blossoming into womanhood. Many men were attracted to her but her relationships were short-lived and disappointing. They lacked the fullness and completeness that she knew was possible if she could only find the one meant for her. Throughout all of her travels, she was looking, searching and seeking, hoping to find him.

One day, she heard about a very wise man with whom many had consulted and found assistance and direction. She inquired about where he lived and was told that he lived on another continent in a very large city amidst the poorest of the poor. She was determined to go wherever necessary to seek his help.

At last, she found herself knocking at his door. A man with sparkling black eyes and a warm smile opened the door. He lived in very primitive conditions. There was no electricity, phone, or running water. He greeted her by name and said he had been expecting her. She was amazed since she had never communicated with him before. She told him her story and made her request.

"Dear One," he said, "I have selected an ancient crystal just for you. Take it with you and in your quiet moments hold it close to you and see what happens.'' He held in his hands a beautiful quartz crystal about three inches long with perfect tips and flawless sides. Anne Marie had never seen such a beautiful crystal before. As she studied it, she sensed an aliveness about it.

As the man placed the stone in her hands, she experienced an activation and at once felt an affinity for it as if it were part of her. Somehow it made her feel complete. She asked the man what she owed him and he answered that he had no needs and that she had already paid him in full by receiving his help. She thanked him and left.

She had traveled halfway around the world to acquire this help and was eager to return to her home. On her journey back she kept the crystal in her purse. She still felt the completeness when she touched the stone. All the unrest of her search seemed to have vanished.

When at last she reached her dwelling, she quickly opened the door and went immediately to her meditation room. She picked up a small medicine bag, a gift from many years ago from a friend who visited Yucatan. The crystal fit perfectly inside the bag. It was almost as if the little pouch had been made to protect that particular crystal. She hung the medicine bag around her neck and the crystal came to rest over her heart. She shut her eyes and went into complete reverie.

At first, she saw colors swirling around, and then a person came into view—a young man with dark hair, brown eyes, and bronzed skin was walking toward her. She recognized him immediately and knew who he was. They embraced—an embrace, which spanned the centuries—at last complete, united, and whole.

"What is your name?" she asked.

"Martu," he replied, "And how are you now called?"

"Anne Marie," she answered.

There was really no need for words. Somehow they knew and understood one another totally—beyond spoken language. The telephone rang and Anne Marie's reverie with her companion stopped immediately, thrusting her back into time and space.

Anne Marie always wore the medicine bag containing the crystal around her neck. Every day, in her quiet moments, she contacted Martu. They had wondrous moments together filled with joy and ecstasy. She wanted Martu to join her in her world, apart from the Crystal Kingdom, but he told her that this was impossible.

As time passed, he told her that when Atlantis was being destroyed, they were separated and later she was drowned as Atlantis was sinking into the ocean. He and many others who practiced the Law of One entered the Crystal Kingdom, each one taking up residence in their individual crystal. They had the technology to take their physical bodies with them and merge with the crystal matrix. Their DNA and physical bodies would be protected from any nuclear or extraterrestrial disasters. They set the time for emergence at 2150 A.D. for they knew at this point Planet Earth would be prepared for their return. This was a code that could not be broken until that eventful date.

Anne Marie wanted to be with Martu all the time. Since it was not possible for him to join her, she wanted to unite with him in the crystal. Martu never encouraged her to do this, as he wanted her to make the choice, to decide independently upon her destiny. She gave deep thought to this, as she knew there was much involved. The decision to be with Martu would be irreversible. After exploring all the possibilities, she chose freely with full knowledge to join Martu in the crystal. Martu was delighted.

He told Anne Marie that the crystal belonged in an ancient temple in Yucatan. The temple still existed but was in bad shape due to centuries of neglect. It was located in a remote site untouched by the modern world. Anne Marie knew that she must travel to the ancient temple and began to put all of her belongings and papers in order, for she knew that she would never return.

She felt certain that she was doing what was right. Her soul longed to be with Martu totally.

If she decided against this, she would die long before Martu could be released from the crystal. There would then be no guarantees that she would ever be able to be with him again. By entering the crystal, she could emerge with Martu in 2150 A.D.

Martu told her that the only reason he could be with her now in her meditations was that the man who gave her the crystal had activated it due to her request. Once she reunited with him, they would be in suspended animation, a more-or-less frozen state, until the release date. Anne Marie would have done anything to preserve their love. She made plans to travel to Yucatan. She knew she would be guided to the right place and besides, she could always consult with Martu. Was she very brave or very foolish to trade her life for a questionable future? Only time would tell.

When Anne Marie stepped off the plane in Yucatan, she knew that there would be no turning back. She had a slight twinge of doubt but her love for Martu overcame it and it never returned. After her meditation the next day, she took a bus to a remote village where Martu instructed her to wait for a guide who would take her into the jungle to the temple. As she got off the bus, she saw some small dwellings with children, chickens, and goats all running freely. Soon people came out to look at her. She could not speak the language so she just smiled and waved. She waited patiently. It was hot and humid and her medicine bag became wet with her perspiration.

At last, she saw a small, middle-aged man coming toward her. His black eyes sparkled. As he came into view, he reminded her of the man that gave her the crystal. He motioned for her to come. She knew he was the person who would guide her to the temple. She felt perfectly safe.

The jungle was alive with animal sounds, vividly colored flowers, and bright green foliage. Birds and butterflies darted everywhere and monkeys chattered overhead in the treetops. It took them seven days of travel to reach their destination. During the last four days, there were no human beings in sight. Anne Marie forded streams and rivers and climbed hills and mountains. Her guide protected her and provided her with food and water. Her excitement increased each day, for soon she would be united totally with her soul mate, Martu.

At last, she saw what appeared to be an old temple. There was moss growing on it and there were many stones that had fallen from the structure and were half buried in the soft earth.

She could hardly wait. Her guide summoned her. He held up his hand for her to stop at the entrance. He went in and disappeared for about 15 minutes, which seemed like an eternity to Anne Marie. The guide reappeared and motioned to her to follow him. There was a false bottom in the temple. He lifted up a few stones, exposing a hole and some stairs. He and Anne Marie squeezed through the hole and walked slowly down the stairs, which led into a series of tunnels.

At the end of the third tunnel, there was a huge slab of rock that looked as if it would require a bulldozer to move it. Her guide emitted a tone at a very high pitch and shortly the stone started to move. When the opening was large enough for Anne Marie and the guide to pass through, they entered into a room. Anne Marie thought she detected some strange etheric music, but she couldn't be sure. The room seemed to glow.

The guide lit a torch. Anne Marie gasped at the beauty. In the center of the room was a huge pyramid covered with sparkling crystals— hundreds of them. It looked as if each crystal was also lighted from within. The crystal in her medicine bag was the same size and shape as all the other crystals.

Anne Marie reached into her medicine bag and gently took out the crystal. She handed it to the guide. She trusted him totally. Her heart was beating fast. She was so close to uniting with Martu, but she knew she must now calm down and concentrate.

The guide looked deeply into her eyes and this time he uttered a lower pitched tone and kept it steady. Her consciousness left her and all that remained were her clothes and the medicine pouch on the floor of the room. She was now united with Martu inside the crystal. The guide gently and lovingly placed the crystal in the only remaining space in the pyramid—the space from which it had recently been removed. Somewhere, deep in the Yucatan, there is an ancient temple where people from long ago are kept in crystals in a state of suspended animation—waiting for the year 2150 A.D. when they will emerge—the year that the whole of humanity on Planet Earth willingly returns and lives according to the will of their Creator.

The Inventor

James loved to tinker with things. Even as a young child, he would build structures for hours while other children were running around and playing all day. At four years old he was able to take his grandfather's watch apart and reassemble it so that it worked. No one could understand where he had learned how to figure this out. When they asked him, James always replied, "I just know and I don't know why."

He spent hours listening to his grandpa tell

him stories. He enjoyed mythology and one of his favorite tales was about Daedalus and Icarus, who created wings for themselves out of bird feathers and wax. However, Icarus flew too close to the sun, which melted the wax on his man-made wings and caused him to fall to his death. James asked for this story frequently.

When James turned seven, his interests were focused primarily on computers. He understood them without being taught. He could take them apart and put them back together. Soon he was repairing the computers of his family members, friends, neighbors, and even his teachers. The principal of his school always asked James to check out a problem computer before hiring a repair person. James saved the school a huge amount of money.

During those years, his father built him a special work area in the basement, where James spent most of his time repairing digital objects and also inventing new ones. By the time he was twelve he had several patents to his name and already had created enough income to finance his college education.

As he continued to experiment, he remembered the story of Daedalus and Icarus. A desire started to grow in James's heart. It was to create some sort of flying apparatus that would be dependable for humans to use individually. This idea grew into a passion of his. He never revealed any of this to a living soul but he felt his schooling and household duties were an inconvenience, for they took up his valuable time, which he thought could have been better spent on his research project.

He loved inventing very small but powerful digital objects. One day, he was inspired to create a device that would be able to transport an object through the air. This was the beginning of his revolutionary flying machine, a device never before seen on Planet Earth. He attached his tiny device to a pencil and hit the go button, but the weight of it caused the pencil to crash to the floor and his invention broke into pieces.

James was not the least bit disturbed. He quickly made another machine, tested it, and it failed. He kept this process up for a few years. He had a certainty about him. He racked up numerous failures but he never wavered in his knowingness that he would be successful in his endeavor. Nothing could dissuade him or discourage him from pursuing this project. In fact, he knew that he knew that he knew in his heart of hearts that he was born to do this work. He was very clear that he was to birth this new technology on Planet Earth. Each time he repeated these experiments he felt even more enthusiasm, for he learned from each mistake how to create a better product.

After some years he was able to make toys that could fly. However, he had to control them with a very small, watch-like device on his wrist. These became popular with his friends but James wanted to create a one person flying apparatus that was capable of moving an individual from one place to another. As James continued his work, he did not want to take the time to attend college. So, instead, the professors came to him, but not to teach him. They came to learn from him.

As James experimented, he finally decided to create a belt -a lightweight flying belt so people could fly wherever and whenever they pleased. By the time James was eighteen, he actually had created a belt that worked, but not for long distances. He could attach it to himself and was able to lift himself up to fly around his basement. He was so excited to at last discover how to be able to lift off and guide himself without bumping into any objects. He combined many different technologies in his belt including sonar, lasers, fiber optics, GPS devices, magnets, crystals, solar energy, and sacred geometry.

After this success, he started testing his flying belt outside. Through perfecting this device, he was able to fly from one hilltop to another. He always took his belt back to his lab to continue improving it. He wanted to create a belt that needed no fuel and one that could go extremely long distances and attain tremendous heights. At last, he built a model that fulfilled these requirements.

The first people to use these were doctors

who would be able to fly to anyone needing help anywhere in the world. After administering emergency treatment, the doctors would be able to attach a belt to the patient and fly them to a clinic. These belts were a phenomenon and highly successful. The belt was then made available for people to travel on their own to places of interest on the Planet. Again he modified and upgraded the belt for this purpose. People were ecstatic.

However, James would not let up his research until he found a way for human beings to travel to other planets and galaxies. By the time James was nearing old age, he at last discovered how to create a galactic belt. He was beside himself with joy. He called it the Orion Belt. It was reserved for a very few explorers of outer space. They were required to complete an intensive program of study before they were allowed to fly on their missions. The Orion Belt was a huge achievement. As a result of James' hard work, a new mythology was created. It was called the Universal Galactic Mythology of Understanding and Peace.

Thank you, James, for being an out of the box thinker. You followed your own music and made your dreams come true to bless humanity.

Oceana,
Mermaid of the Great Waters

Oceana was small but amazingly powerful. She was the Mermaid Princess of the Great Waters, which contained all of the oceans and seas on Planet Earth. She loved this water world filled with electric blues, greens, and turquoise hues which danced and swirled continuously, creating whiter than white foam cresting on its waves. The water was a living substance that sparkled with Life and Light. Oceana played endlessly in this liquid crystalline wonder world. Her iridescent tail flipped and waved to and fro as she swam and dove down to the depths and then suddenly sprang up to the surface, only to submerge herself once again.

She would race with the Fish People and then dart and hide among the corals and sea anemones to see if any of them were fast enough to find her. All the creatures of the Great Waters loved her. She was their leader and led them with compassion and great wisdom. All sea creatures, both plant and animal, bowed to her desires which were always for the Highest Good of everyone. Just her presence would bring calm, harmony, joy, and understanding.

Oceana's favorite playmate was Skylar, the seahorse. She loved riding him and fit perfectly onto his back. As her hands gently but firmly encircled his neck, his stained-glass like wings would begin beating in rhythm with his heart in preparation for takeoff. They could literally fly through the water. Often they were seen laughing with glee as they turned summersaults and danced their way through their liquid wonder world. They were able to take off at a moment's notice to help out in any emergency situation that arose. Skylar loved taking Princess Oceana on his back and felt greatly honored that she had selected him to assist her.

When Oceana wasn't rushing off to solve problems, she would swim and frolic with the dolphins. Their clicking and antics always made her laugh until she thought her sides would burst. Her laughter spread out all over the Great Waters and brought untold joy and happiness to all its inhabitants.

Another pastime that Oceana loved was swimming to the surface to perch on a rock or a piece of floating wood and take a sunbath or just admire the sky and the clouds. Her iridescent tail would sparkle in the sun rays, attracting Those Who Flew in the Air. They would keep their distance out of respect. In return, Oceana would share with them the Mysteries of the Deep. This filled the Beings of the Air to overflowing with gratitude. They always looked forward to her visits with the Air World.

Not only was Oceana an outstanding problem solver, but she was also an artist. She was given the Gift of Art. When a new species of sea creature or ocean plant was brought forth, she was given the assignment of painting them with their permanent coloring, adding sheen and their specific imprint or design. This imprint was actually their energetic signature that enabled them to create their own tone and harmony in the Symphony of the Great Waters. Their designs contained hidden codes that could be activated at specific times to create more beautiful harmonies and myriad shades of radiant colors. This was Oceana's favorite task. Her creations made the ocean inhabitants just as colorful if not more so than those Beings living on Land.

Under the surface, you could hear the Symphony of the Great Waters. This is how Oceana could detect when there was a problem because the music would become discordant. When she heard even the slightest discord, she would jump on the back of Skylar and speed away to correct the situation. Upon their arrival, they were able to harmonize the discord before it became unmanageable.

Many years ago, humans, who had lost their connection with the Source of All started polluting the Great Waters with poisons from their own waste, chemicals, fuels, and trash. Eventually, everything in the Great Waters became ill and started dying. Oceana and Skylar wept tears of sadness, as did all the other Beings who lived in the Waters. It was difficult for them to see through all the pollution and the music started to sound extremely discordant. Oceana and Skylar were exhausted because their services were in constant demand.

Soon the Great Waters could no longer feed the air its water vapor, and it stopped raining over the Earth. Humans, animals, and plants of the Land started dying of thirst. Without water nothing could survive. Water was one of the most sacred elements essential for Life. In fact, most Beings were primarily water. As this condition worsened, the Great Waters tried to warn humanity by creating unusual flooding of the land all over the Earth. The weight of the pollution caused the Earth's crust under the Great Waters to explode and the force of these explosions created tsunamis. All of this resulted in great tragedy but nonetheless, humans continued polluting the Great Waters.

Princess Oceana sent out a clarion call to all Beings within the Deep to assemble. It was urgent that something be done before the Great Waters were no longer able to give Life to their inhabitants. When Oceana put forth the call, representatives from every type of Water Being came to the meeting, from the largest whale down to the smallest microscopic plant and animal. To begin the meeting, Oceana requested silence and that they focus on the Source of All Creation in gratitude for their life and ask how they could help reverse the tragedy of pollution. A great hush fell on the gathering as they gave thanks from their heart of hearts and put forth their appeal.

After a very long silence, they shared what they had heard in the deep recesses of their hearts. The result was that they focused love messages into the hearts of humans to come to their aid and help resolve this crisis. At the end of the meeting, they all felt they had made successful contact and agreed and decreed that positive change would be manifested, expanded, and prevail. To conclude the gathering, they sent up another great surge of appreciation, love, and gratitude to the Source of All Creation from their heart of hearts beating together as One. For the first time in millennia, there was once again a conscious bond that formed between humans and the Beings in the Great Waters. After that, they left to go back to their respective territories.

The very next day, all over Planet Earth, small groups of people started coming to the shores of the Great Waters offering prayers, songs from their hearts, and ceremonies straight from Mother Earth and Great Spirit to all the Beings that lived therein and to the crystalline structure of the Water Itself. Little by little the humans' love and devotion to this task grew into a huge movement which covered the Earth. The Great Waters started to clear. It started to rain again. The humans polluting the water realized with horror the error of their ways and they resolved to stop, one by one.

This Work took almost ten years to complete until today, anyone can look into the Great Waters and see clearly the Beings living there. If they are lucky they can catch a glimpse of Princess Oceana riding on Skylar or sunbathing in the Air World. Now that the communication has opened up, Great Water Beings, Humans, and other Land Beings can understand one another. Their hearts beat together in harmony as One in the Great Collective. Once again, the Great Waters sparkle with Living Energies and Light. Its crystalline structure is renewed and has returned to its pristine blueprint. Life, health, and well-being are now available to all living forms on Planet Earth.

No matter where you are, you can ask Princess Oceana and Skylar if they will take you on a ride in the Great Waters when you enter dreamland. And you can always send the neverending supply of love from your heart into all the hearts of every living Being in the Great Waters and to the very water itself. This way you, too, can help keep the water pure and sparkling clear. This is very important Work and anyone of any age can do this.

Thank you, Water, for your precious Gift to all of us.

The Prince

Once upon a time, there was a handsome prince who had all the material gifts a man could ever want but nonetheless he felt an emptiness. He had a tremendous yearning, which nothing seemed to satisfy.

He was a very deep thinker and while always cheerful to all, he was given to taking long walks alone so that he could pursue his thoughts without interruption. It was on one of these journeys that he met an old man who told him of a very special place where he could visit to be able to think with much more clarity. The old man went on to say that very few people found this place, for around it was an impenetrable shield. Only those whose natures were in tune with the Higher Life could pass through the invisible wall. The old man told the prince that the way to find this spot was to concentrate on his desire to be there. The prince thanked the man and placed in his hands a pouch containing sixteen coins made of pure gold.

After the conversation with the old man, the prince focused his attention on this place and felt as if he were being transported through the air. When he landed, he knew where he was and walked through the shield just as the old man had described to him. He was struck with awe at the wonder therein. Before him were beautiful mountain peaks capped with snow, trees, flowers, waterfalls, bubbling brooks, birds-all of an unusual quality—that of eternal spring.

A golden shaft of light pierced through to the prince's heart, and for the first time in his life, he felt truly alive. His thoughts became clearer and he discovered that no longer was his brain the originator of his thinking, but someone was speaking to him the truth of truths from the innermost depths of himself. He then became a listener and the yearning within him began to lessen. Time came for him to return to his principality. People seemed to note a difference in the prince. He still was cheerful but he seemed to take on a radiant quality and his eyes appeared like deep pools.

He frequently returned to this mystic glade in the wood. Each visit filled him with joy and beauty of untold depth. He learned to listen to the plants and animals. They all told him their stories and thoughts and in return, he spoke with them. He learned that God loves everything equally, for there is a spark of the Divine in all that lives. When he attuned himself to this spark, all secrets were revealed. His eyes saw with true vision and his ears were filled with celestial melodies.

Each time the prince returned to his kingdom, the people felt a deeper change in him. He was transformed from a young man into a person of great wisdom and depth. His love grew to such an extent that mothers whose children were crying or sick would bring their ailing ones to him to hold. Their children became well and calm again and as the prince held them, they exchanged smiles. The face of the prince was like the sun and the children like thirsty flowers drank in his radiance and in turn, they blossomed forth.

One day, the prince experienced such painstaking beauty in his sacred glade that he fell into a trance in which he dreamed a long dream of many, many centuries. In this dream, he saw himself living through many lives -an Egyptian slave, a Greek artist, a medieval wizard, a cruel despot, a Spanish explorer, a gypsy dancer, a crippled old woman, a deaf mute, a sharecropper, a wealthy businessman, until at last he awakened and found himself once more seated upon a stone by a brook in the sacred glade. He felt older and wiser than ever before.

The shaft of golden light pierced his heart once more. He became fully aware and saw the Work that lay ahead of him, the long years of service, and the endless time before he would be able to return permanently to his true home.

The Weaver

When Katelyn was a tiny little girl, she loved to play with the naturally dyed balls of yarn that her mother made on the spinning wheel. She would sit at her mother's feet and listen to the birds singing and to the spinning wheel as it spun the wool while she played with the colorful yarn. She would entertain herself in this way as her mother wove beautiful rugs, wall hangings, tapestries, and garments.

Her mother used the wool from sheep,

alpacas, and lamas. Katelyn loved lama wool most of all. It was so soft and cuddly. She begged her mother to weave her a blanket. When her mother finished it, Katelyn was so excited. She loved the blanket and slept and cuddled with it every day for the rest of her life.

They lived in a hilly farm area away from the city. There were woods close by and mountains in the distance. Katelyn spent most of her days collecting eggs from the chickens, milking the goats, romping with their cats and dogs, and playing with her imaginary friends. She was in love with the natural world. Among the highlights of her childhood was going into the wilds with her mother to collect the leaves, flowers, fruits, and roots of particular plants to dye the wool.

As Katelyn grew older, she took great

pleasure in spinning and weaving her own creations. Every Saturday Katelyn and her mother would take their work from the week to sell at the open market in the city. People would flock to their booth. Within a short time, everything they had made was snatched up by eager buyers. Customers raved about their remarkable work.

Katelyn noticed there was an old woman watching her every time she was in the booth. The woman had a kind face which always held a smile. Her eyes sparkled and she seemed to emit a delicate, gold light around her person. They never spoke but just smiled at one another when their eyes met. Katelyn felt like she knew her but couldn't quite remember where they had met. The woman never purchased anything but just remained quiet and peaceful in the background.

As Katelyn matured, her weaving advanced to higher levels of artistry. She started using very tiny threads of pure gold in her pieces. The gold would sparkle through the colored wool, creating a field of light which emanated from her work. Her creations were in such demand that soon the wealthiest people in the area came from miles around to the market just to buy her art.

Katelyn had a life-changing dream on the night she turned 16. The old woman she had seen for years at the market came to her in dreamtime. She seemed to be sparkling all over. The woman gave her a tiny golden seed shaped like a hexagon and a small goblet filled with nectar. The seed was not of this Earth. It contained a new technology which gave Katelyn the alchemical ability to fuse thought to matter. Katelyn carefully took the seed and placed it on her tongue. Then she lifted the goblet to her lips and swallowed the seed along with the delicious nectar. Instantly, the seed turned into a type of liquid gold and merged with the mitochondria of every cell in her body.

When she awoke from her dream, she could not wait to weave her next creation. She fell in love with the world and everyone she came in contact with. No matter what happened to her, she never closed her heart and was able to maintain her inner joy.

As she continued her weaving, people who bought her work noticed that their lives started changing for the better. They would come back to the market to tell her what miracles her weaving was accomplishing. This news thrilled Katelyn and filled her with gratitude. The reputation of her artwork spread like wildfire.

Before long she was being asked by cities, counties, and states to create tapestries for them to hang on their walls, not only to beautify their buildings but more importantly to harmonize the environment and all who were in it. As Katelyn spun and wove her pieces, she would envision hearts opening up, harmony, kindness, honesty, compassion, and generosity. These qualities were alchemically embedded within the golden threads and radiated outward continuously.

Word spread over the Earth about Katelyn's tapestries and she was busy creating wall hangings for governments and kingdoms all over the Globe. Through this work, Great Harmony penetrated through to the leaders of people. They started to lead with kindness, compassion, integrity, and generosity. Renewal was the thought in everyone's mind. The heaviness on the Planet lifted. People began to breathe and laugh again. Peace was now a possibility and within reach.

Follow your heart and your gifts will develop beyond your wildest dreams.

The Seed

One day, as Christopher was walking through the woodland, he was enraptured by the surrounding beauty and came upon a meadow. He sat down on a log and was entranced by the scene. Before him lay a panorama of flowers dancing with joy, trees bending over them, bees and other insects bringing the hum of other worlds into their midst, butterflies rejoicing in their freedom and sharing their exuberance with the denizens of the meadow.

There in the far corner, Christopher saw a doe and her fawn drinking from a quiet pool. For Christopher it was as if he were seeing for the first time, for he realized how all these Beings were working in harmony and communicating with one another. It was as if he were watching a symphony and he was caught up with a sound of splendor which he could not yet hear but felt more deeply than he had ever felt anything before. He experienced an expansion of his Being and he cried tears of knowingness. If only he could share this with others.

As Christopher sat there just Being— another member of the scene, playing his part, his melody, the doe and fawn seemed to lose all shyness and came over to him.

He could almost hear them speak and it was as if they said, "Welcome, Little Brother, your vibration adds a beautiful harmony to our meadow. Thank you for Being. Come anytime.'' Christopher in amazement said quietly, ''Thank you for inviting me into your home. It is absolutely glorious and the most sublime experience I have ever had. I would like to bring others here.''

''Yes, we know, Christopher, but they are not ready. They must reach a point of calmness within themselves first, or become so very weary of their doings that they begin to desire another way. It must be a sincere desire and one to create something greater within themselves.'' ''Have you ever met our teacher?'' ''No,'' said Christopher.

''You probably have in your dreams, but now the time has come for you to meet him in your conscious state. You see, we are all his students and are here to do his work, which is to evolve as much as we can in the time allotted to us.''

Christopher looked up and there in the far corner of the meadow was a brilliant Light. Its radiance was blinding and the Sound that issued from it was sheer ecstasy. Christopher felt so much love enter into his Being that he actually hurt. All the plants and animals became very still, for their teacher had come to speak. All got the message. All heard what they needed to hear. He filled each ones' cup to overflowing so that they would have enough to feed upon until his next appearance.

To Christopher, he said, ''Welcome to the Garden. I'm glad you made the choice to come. I know your desire and it is a very noble one. I am giving you a seed but you are not to plant it until you come to the right place. You will travel widely, the seed will protect you and you will know when to plant it, for a great power will carry you up to the heights and you will be filled with ecstasy. It is then that you will plant the seed in total awareness of what you are doing.''

It was true. Christopher became a young man and he ventured forth, experimenting with life, even at times forgetting his goal, but growing wise through his experiences. Many times, he was careless with himself and felt no longer worthy to be a carrier of the seed. He had many dark adventures, some of untold rapture, and many years of humdrum in-between. One thing Christopher did not realize was that the seed was ripening and unfolding as he was maturing. Each experience added another facet to the seed and gave it greater understanding, greater beauty. At times, Christopher felt the seed as a great burden upon him and at other times he felt humbled having been chosen to be a carrier.

At last, one day Christopher came upon a village where the people were filled with despair, for they had seen their small empire collapse through their own greed and selfishness. The young no longer had any ambition, for even before they learned to talk they knew their elders were sick in spirit and that they no longer had ideals but were blindly wandering about like babes whimpering in the wilderness, destroying the last vestiges of hope in an effort to feed themselves. The beasts of the field were dying of neglect and disease.

When Christopher was among them, he knew where he was and had compassion for these dear lost ones, for he, too, had experienced what they were experiencing and had known the sheer hopelessness of the error of his ways. He felt that the people had been crying deep within themselves for a very long time. Their village was a wasteland and most were in a stupor, trying to forget their actions and the state to which they had reduced themselves.

Standing there, Christopher felt a great power raise him up. He became filled with ecstasy and Light. He then knew he was to plant the seed at this very place. The first words Christopher spoke were, "Dear Ones, I have come to give you hope." The people made an effort to gather round him. Slowly, they felt life flow into them and their tears came from deep within and spilled onto the ground.

The tears were of remorse and joy and watered the thirsty earth. As Christopher spoke to them of the Garden he had seen long ago and of the seed he came to plant in their village, their stupor left, their eyes became clear and aware. He told them they must work together to nourish the seed, for if there were not harmony, this would affect its growth.

These people had known the dire poverty of spirit and now they were given a chance to enter into life once more. With deep gratitude and awareness of their real nature, they rejoiced as they watched Christopher plant the seed in their midst. As he did so, a brilliant light appeared and the people and animals were transported to the very heights of ecstasy by a wave of glory, a silent symphony. It was at that moment that they truly accepted the seed and the responsibility that went with it.

"And now, Blessed Ones, you have had a taste of reality, your true nature and your true home. When the seed matures and bears fruit, you are to eat the fruit, but keep the seed. By that time, you will be ready to go out among others and do for them as I have done for you.''

From that day on, the people began to work together in harmony and joy. They had a goal and that was to create a beautiful garden, which would draw to it and awaken the nobility, which lay deep in all Beings. They began anew and tilled the soil. It was work of a higher nature and more rewarding than anything they had ever known.

She Who Breathes

Sky loved the breath, even as a child. She would breathe in the air slowly, deeply, and gently. She would feel it fill her belly and lungs to capacity and then she would breathe out fully, feeling how delicious it was to just breathe in and then breathe out. It was so simple and yet so wonderfully satisfying.

Everywhere Sky went, she would breathe this way. It was so freeing for her spirit and no one ever could notice that she was doing anything out of the ordinary. This was her secret and her delight. As she got older, she discovered that she could breathe in the essence of anything she desired. For example, she loved flowers and especially the Lily of the Valley. She would breathe in its fragrance and fully enjoy it and then breathe it out into the world to help detoxify harmful negative substances and thoughts.

She would walk through an herb garden and breathe in the essence of the herbs she loved. They would heal whatever needed healing in her body and then she would breathe the essences out to go to other people who needed them, many confined to their beds at home or in the hospital.

Sky never worried about food. In fact, she had no need or desire to eat. She could go into a garden or an open market and breathe in the essence of those foods her body was drawn to that particular day. In this way, her body absorbed the nutrients it needed to stay in top condition. It was her delight to just sit in a garden and absorb the vibrant colors of the flowers and breathe these frequencies into the cells of her body and then breathe them out to nourish the world.

She realized that everything had a rhythm, a breath, but so subtle that you would have to be very patient and observant to witness this. Even the Earth, the moon, the sun, the Milky Way breathed in and out. In fact, the whole of the Universe is shaped like a donut, a torus, with never ending circulation of energy that moves in a rhythm-like breath. The breath is connected to the heart. Without the breath, the heart stops. Without Breath, there is no life.

Sky would begin each day by breathing in the Light from the Central Sun and streaming it down through her crown chakra, continuing through the center of her body and exhaling it out the soles of her feet, descending down to the Light deep inside the core of Mother Earth. Then she would inhale this Light back up into her body through the soles of her feet following the same pathway up through her body and breathing it out her crown chakra back to the Central Sun. This practice connected her with Above and Below and created a calm within her that allowed her to merge with the Now of each day and remain balanced and energized.

She especially loved the trees. When she touched a tree, she felt an immediate connection with Heaven and Earth. The trees seem to be in meditation with their breath and Gaia's breath all day. Sky realized they were the lungs of the Earth, so to speak. Their trunks and branches resembled our respiratory system. The trees breathed in carbon dioxide and breathed out oxygen. Humans would breathe in the oxygen from the trees, which they required to live, and then breathe out carbon dioxide, which the trees needed for their life. What an intricate symbiotic relationship and a masterful plan! We cannot live without the trees and they cannot live without us.

Sky loved her breath. For her, it was a sacrament, a Gift that she gave freely, her closest companion, and friend for life.

Be conscious of your breath. Let it nourish you and take you into states of ecstasy and delight. Listen to the Breath of Gaia and breathe with Her.

The Builder

Kai loved to build. As a child, she occupied her time with tinker toys, Lincoln Logs, Legos, and blocks. From there she graduated to forts and tree houses. She was fascinated how other life forms built their shelters: bird nests, ant hills, bear dens, spider webs. All creating beautiful spaces for themselves out of natural materials.

As she matured, she explored how humans from other cultures built their homes: cliff dwellers, Eskimos, Native Americans,

Mongolians, Pacific Islanders, Egyptians, Africans, and South American tribes. She studied the sod houses in Europe, Earthships in New Mexico, geodesic domes, and sculpted houses made out of straw bale and clay from the Earth.

By the time Kai was a young woman, she had accumulated a vast store of knowledge. Her brain contained the most comprehensive compilation of architecture known to man from the beginning of civilization down to the present time. Her desire was to create houses individuated specifically for each person. She realized that our first and foremost home was our body and that everyone's body was their unique architecture.

Kai studied math, astronomy, art, engineering, physics, music, landscape design, herbal medicine, physiology, and genetics. She was an avid eclectic learner and her genius absorbed, synthesized, and assimilated all this knowledge. She was particularly fascinated with the Fibonacci sequence, the properties of water, fractals, free energy, and sacred geometry. Her passion to free the souls of people and to help facilitate their return to full consciousness influenced and became the driving force behind her architectural designs.

She incorporated everything she learned into her blueprints. Her buildings were inspired and each successive one was more amazing than the last. Kai's creations were organic, holistic structures built in conscious harmony with the Universe. They formed a living structure in which humans, animals, and plants thrive and receive healthy, viable energies that are transmitted to them continuously from the design, technologies, and the materials used.

These energies activated codes within the visitors and inhabitants that helped them unfold into Greater Awareness.

Each day she awoke, she could not wait to create her next design. Each home was unique and bore her energetic signature. As word spread of her talent and genius, she received commissions from all over Planet Earth to build museums, libraries, universities, concert halls, housing clusters, observatories, etc. There was no way Kai could complete all the work that was offered her.

Her creations were not just containers for people to be in. They were actually more like multidimensional forms and musical instruments that would 'clothe' and 'caress' the occupants, almost like a second skin. They were made of many shapes: circles, octagons, triangles, tetrahedrons, diamonds, and as many more as you could imagine. The designs were mathematically so advanced that they connected Earth with the astral or multidimensional field. They emitted music that would change according to what beings were present inside the structure. People or animals inside these buildings harmonized with the Music of the Spheres.

In spite of their variations of form, these buildings functioned as antennas all over the surface of Earth. These antennas brought energies through them, which formed harmonic shields, which in turn created rainbow-like prisms connecting Heaven with Earth. In fact, all the structures connected ethereally and created a Golden Grid over the surface of Gaia. Hearts opened. People awakened out of their deep sleep. They recognized their Greatness, their multidimensionality. They were filled with

Oneness, unconditional love, and peace. The Earth and all its inhabitants became a glorious symphony, each one contributing to the whole and harmonizing as they played their own songs.

Jeremy

Jeremy was a collector of just about everything that anyone could possibly collect. He began this activity as most of us did in childhood. However, the difference was that he never narrowed his interests and never stopped collecting. He continued being the reservoir for all things within his sphere wherever he was functioning at the time.

This hobby completely absorbed Jeremy's every moment. He could no longer discipline himself to stop collecting, for he had given into the enormity of this habit years ago. It follows to reason that Jeremy's lifestyle would be rather unusual due to the broad scope of his interests.

Jeremy was a very lovable person and developed over the years into a hobo of sorts. He traveled around in a big wagon shaped like a boat. He had designed and built a tricycle in the very center and when he desired to move, he peddled his tricycle. He had placed a calliope over the tricycle wheels so that he could play it as he moved. Covering the whole contraption was a huge polka dotted umbrella. Sticking out in plain view was his shingle, which stated: JEREMY. GENERALIST, PUTTERER, AND COLLECTOR OF THE SEEN AND THE UNSEEN. SELF-EMPLOYED.

Now Jeremy had no choice anymore but to collect. He could never work at anything specific, for he spent most of his time collecting, sorting, cataloging, and reviewing. Sorting meant rearranging, never casting out. As he added new things, he would have to start from the beginning of his collection and review the whole works again and catalogue the most recent item in its proper place. This constituted incredible amounts of energy and time. Not that Jeremy minded all this, for it kept him very busy and you might say "entertained." He was never bored and acquired the reputation for being a hard worker. Everyone just assumed that he was engaged in some very important endeavor.

Often at night he would lay awake, his heart beating wildly, wondering about his belongings and reviewing his collection mentally. The only problem was that he had very little free attention, to say the least. Many times, old friends or new acquaintances would stop by and invite Jeremy to go to a party or for a train ride or just anything to get him off his wagon, but he never went. The main reason was that he couldn't let go of his collecting, cataloging, sorting, and reviewing and he surely couldn't leave his wagon, for something might disappear. He even had to adjust his hours of sleep so that he had more sorting time and less sleeping time.

Jeremy had devised a unique form of record keeping. This was of necessity, for over the years his brain would become riveted to an object he was cataloging and would keep going over and over it like a broken answering machine. This cost Jeremy dearly in terms of time. He tried out many ideas to prevent this vexation, but none worked until he thought of using glockenspiels. He placed one at each end of his boat. He trained himself to go to the closest glockenspiel and hit one of the bars (which sound like bells), thus marking the end of that particular cycle on that particular object and at the same time freeing his attention for the next item to be processed. Often times for days, the only sounds that issued forth from Jeremy's place were shuffling, rattling, tugging, pushing, and shoving, all punctuated throughout by the bells of the glockenspiel.

On occasion, when he felt burdened down with his collection, he would play the calliope and the birds, people, and animals would come from miles around mainly just to observe Jeremy in one of his rare moments of boundless joy and freedom. This was the only time Jeremy didn't collect, sort, catalogue, or review. However, the minute he stopped playing, collecting started at once and all the people, animals, and birds hurried away during the last strains of the music so they wouldn't become part of his collection. Some weren't fast enough and Jeremy collected parts of them, too, but mainly just the painful parts and they seemed strangely better.

It was getting more and more difficult for Jeremy to travel around due to the enormous quantities of boxes, bags, and bangles he acquired over the years. He also needed more room for sorting, as he never threw anything away and certainly never gave anything away, for it would alter the structure too much. He knew that collecting was ruining him, trapping him, and he even had nightmares from time to time of having to settle down someday...in a HOUSE! (Just the thought would make Jeremy shudder.)

This became of such great concern to him that he began building a platform—his last attempt to remain mobile. He planned to put all his belongings on the platform and buy a huge balloon and travel around above the ground. His main reason for doing this was to ''get away from it all'' so he wouldn't have to collect anymore, as he already had more than he could cope with. The only problem in his doing this was that he was unable to sort and build at the same time, but he soon discovered a technique whereby he could build and another part of him would just space out and continue to sort, recall, and catalogue his collection.

Jeremy built the platform around his wagon so that he would be able to move the whole affair by peddling his tricycle, if necessary. He bought an enormous orange balloon for the center of his creation. Even after Jeremy packed everything on the platform and wagon, the whole whimsy was bulging and sagging under the weight. There was room for only a very narrow walkway for Jeremy to squeeze by in his daily rounds. At last, he was ready for the take off. It took several days for the platform to rise and then it only rose about three feet off the ground. This was not satisfactory at all and since Jeremy could not throw anything away, he solved the problem, and very well at that, by strapping four more balloons to the platform— one to each corner. As he was taking off, peddling his tricycle, he played his calliope mainly to prevent collecting anything else, but also in celebration of the possibility of ridding of his addiction once and for all.

Up Jeremy went, up over the clouds. Up...up...up...until he remembered -how could he forget!!!—his collection...and with that he stopped his whole whimsy and anchored it on a wish in space. He quit playing the calliope and began ruminating again on his collection.

One day, as he was puttering around, poking and sorting, he heard someone say, "Hi!" He dismissed it, for he had heard stories of how when people get absorbed in their material and are alone a lot they begin to hear voices, so he just felt it was one of THOSE things. Again it said, "Hey, Jeremy, I'm up here." Jeremy chuckled, for he had never heard voices before—and he never dreamed they'd have a sense of humor. Then it spoke a third time, "Jeremy, if you don't look up here I'm going to burst your balloon and you'll be stuck in this place for a long, long time."

That was all Jeremy needed to hear. Up he looked and there he beheld someone way up on his balloon. Jeremy said, "Why hello!" half out of surprise and half out of welcome.

With that, this person somehow projected himself from the balloon to right before

Jeremy's eyes in a split second. Jeremy had never in his whole life met anyone who reminded him more of himself than this person before him now. He even dressed a little bit like Jeremy, but there was a different quality about him that puzzled him until he became aware of what it was: This person was totally free. He had NO COLLECTION!

"Who are you?" asked Jeremy in amazement.

"Are you sure you can take time away from your collection to find out?"

Jeremy laughed, for he could sense that this person knew him very, very well, indeed. And yet, this was not an uncomfortable feeling, for this person knew him, understood him, and loved him more than he did himself.

"What is your name?" asked Jeremy.

"Let's see," said his friend,

"Uh……suppose you call me……..Stuttgart."

With that, they both let go with a warm belly laugh. "You're really something else, Jeremy. I don't think anyone but you could have made it this far with all that baggage you tote around. You must have made it on pure gut determination."

"I've been a collector so long that I think I would really miss it. It's a question of starting out with something and becoming so engrossed with it over such a long period of years that it's part of you and you can't give it up."

"The word 'can't' is not in my vocabulary," stated Stuttgart.

Jeremy scratched his head and chuckled, for he had met his match.

"I haven't met too many collectors with your strength, Jeremy. It's really a miracle that you're still…on top of it. Are you willing to experiment? I'll even watch your collection for you while you go off and see what it feels like to be free."

Jeremy never thought of himself as a miser but it was true that his collection was like gold to him. For example, to lose the piece of chewed chewing gum he had found sticking to his tricycle wheel over fifty years ago would be a loss which would cost him dearly in terms of losing something he had grown used to, something he had learned to love, not to mention the labor of resorting and beginning from the beginning again to catalogue. It's true that Jeremy trusted Stuttgart but it would be awhile and perhaps a long while before he would trust him with his collection. And besides, what interest did he have for anything outside of the collection, anyway.

"What's so great about being free,

Stuttgart? Does it keep you busy—like my work?''

''As long as you collect, you are not free. I will show you, Jeremy, when you are ready.''

Jeremy just shrugged his shoulders and went back to his work, happy that Stuttgart wouldn't bug him anymore about it. Well, there was no need, for Stuttgart's invitation became a part of Jeremy's collection and he reviewed it along with everything else when he reviewed which, as you know by now, was often. Jeremy would keep an eye on Stuttgart to make sure he would not interfere with his collection in any way and to see if he could really trust him.

As for Stuttgart, he would spend a great deal of time sitting on the orange balloon. Sometimes he would do his instant transfer to another balloon and sometimes he would disappear altogether—just vanish. He called these his 'adventures in freedom'. It was true that Jeremy was becoming mildly curious. Stuttgart seemed enthusiastic about everything. He was never bored and appeared to be living a fascinating life. And all this without a collection. Jeremy became more interested.

Finally, one day Jeremy became so curious he couldn't stand it anymore. "Where do you go on your excursions?" he blurted out after hitting the glockenspiel.

"Well," answered Stuttgart, "I make up different worlds and places in my mind and then I go out and explore them."

Jeremy laughed, for Stuttgart always amazed him by answering a question in such a way that it was totally different from what he expected.

"You see, Jeremy, I create my own worlds and they become real and other people can visit them, too. If you ever got rid of your collection, you could do this and we could visit each other's worlds and even make some worlds up together.''

''Is that what being free means?''

''Yes, in part, it means that you can create, come and go as you please, but never collect.''

''But that's your collection—those worlds.'' ''No, I just create, never possess.''

''But doesn't that clutter up space?''

''Oh, no. How much space does an idea occupy?''

Now Jeremy had never entertained thoughts of other worlds or even the one he inhabited, for his collection completely absorbed his total interest. Could it be true that there was something more interesting than his collection? Could he risk the amount of time re-doing his collection if he visited these other places? He knew by now that he could trust Stuttgart, but all Stuttgart could do was guard—not catalogue, sort, or rearrange. In fact, Stuttgart could not even learn how to do this, for it would be entirely against his nature.

Finally, one day, as Jeremy was cataloging some lead piping that he acquired some time ago, he slammed his foot down so hard on the platform that it almost went clear through. "Alright, by golly, I'll do it!" he shouted. "But if something happens to my collection, I'll hold you accountable, Stuttgart!" Then, embarrassed by his own words, he said very meekly, "Teach me?"

With that Stuttgart appeared instantly at Jeremy's side. He was very careful with Jeremy's feelings, for he knew Jeremy was taking a giant step, was feeling very fragile at the time, and would need his firm but gentle guidance for a rather extensive training period. "When have you felt the most free from your collection?"

Jeremy thought and thought some more and then remembered, "When I play the calliope. It's been so long since I've played it I almost forgot."

"Then the first step is to play the calliope every day and keep adding a little more time each day. I will guard your collection while you play, so don't worry. While you're playing, I want you to really get into the feeling of what it's like to be without a collection."

As Jeremy practiced on the calliope, he began to wonder why he hadn't played more often before. He would close his eyes and imagine himself playing instant tag with Stuttgart on the balloons. Instant tag was when you could tag a person and instantly be 50 to 1,000 feet away. Little by little, Jeremy actually began to enjoy this so much that he would even, at times—that is, desire to do this more than work on his collection.

One day, as he was playing with his eyes closed, Stuttgart appeared and invited him to accompany him to the Land of the Purple Boon Bagels. At last, Jeremy was ready to go out exploring. "Stuttgart, I'm ready."

And with that, they instantly found themselves in a very strange place, indeed. They were standing on a hillock watching a sea-green sun appear on the horizon and spread its rays over the golden grass. Jeremy was breathlessly awaiting his first glimpse of a Purple Boon Bagel.

"Now, you must look very carefully for them and in a certain way. You must believe beyond doubt that they are real; otherwise, they will not show themselves to you. In other words, we could be standing together and I could see them and you would not if you had the wrong attitude."

Jeremy now knew why Stuttgart waited so long to take him adventuring, for at all times before this he would have either laughed about the Boon Bagels, making fun of them and not believing that they existed, or he would be extremely afraid of them. Now he was ready and he stood there like a child in wonder and total acceptance of what he was about to see.

Slowly as the aquamarine sun rose, he saw an orange door open on a distant hillock and out of it came—a Purple Boon Bagel. He watched, breathless in amazement. The creature moved about on starfish type tube feet. It moved slowly and rhythmically and seemed to be performing a dance to welcome the sun. It was circular in shape with a hole in the middle.

Soon other orange doors opened and Purple Boon Bagels were popping out all over. Some were rolling around on their sides, others were flipping over and over, more were sliding in circles and others just twirling.

Jeremy was totally entranced with the scene. He wondered if he would be able to communicate with these beings, but Stuttgart informed him that they were invisible to the Boon Bagels. And, indeed, Jeremy looked over at Stuttgart and all he saw was a pair of eyes. He looked at himself and saw NOTHING, but since he could see everything else he deducted that he too was just a pair of eyes.

"That's enough for your first exposure," said Stuttgart, and before Jeremy knew it, he found himself back playing his calliope. It seemed that a lot of time had elapsed, but on the other hand, perhaps it all took place in a second.

He wasn't sure.

''You're confused, Jeremy, because we went into another dimension which is beyond time and space. So just accept the experience but don't catalogue it. You will probably do so out of habit, but until you free it from your collection you will never be able to have another adventure...and you will never be able to explore on your own until you get rid of your collection entirely.''

Final Words

Just the beginning, not the end.
The end is always the beginning
of something else.

"What lies behind us and what lies before us are
tiny matters compared to what lies within us."

— Ralph Waldo Emerson

About the Author

After working many years in the public sector Nadja is reinventing herself as an artist and writer. She has an eclectic background. Her joys include adventuring on the Open Road, dancing, cooking, being in nature, writing and painting. She is also interested in natural building, organic gardening, alternative health, lifelong learning, travel, and living moment to moment. Nadja writes for the conscious community and people who are interested in healing, meditation, transformation, ascension, and the New Earth. This includes highly sensitive people, Starseeds, Indigos, empaths, Light Workers, energy healers, artists, visionaries, and those in recovery and discovery.

Her website is NadjaMedia.com

Also by Nadja

Soft-cover books, eBooks, MP3s, and CDs
Smashwords, Amazon, Kindle, CreateSpace,
CDBaby, iTunes, YouTube, and your local
bookstore by request.

River of Living Light

Evolution Revolution

Random Thoughts and Poems

Hopi Blue Corn

El Maiz Azul de los Hopis

Visionary Tales for the New Earth

Color Me Bright Coloring Book